NOT YETI

WRITTEN BY KELLY DiPUCCHIO
ILLUSTRATED BY CLAIRE KEANE

VIKING

The world is full of monsters.

Some monsters kick.

Some pinch.

And others, like Lumpy Stinker, will hide
rotten egg salad sandwiches in the back
of your sock drawer.

Most monsters are only interested
in being right.
And loud.
And rude.
But not Yeti.
He crochets sweaters
for penguins.

He compliments the weeds
as he passes them by
on his morning walks.

And when he read that humpback whales sing . . .

he rode his scooter to the pier just so
he could sing back to them.

Yeti tried to be friendly with the other monsters.
He brought them warm banana bread.

He made them inspirational quotes to hang on their walls.

He even offered to babysit for free.

Crud. He definitely won't
do that again!

There was a time when Yeti's behavior was downright abominable and he acted a lot like Grimace.

And Itchy Bottom.

And, most regrettably, like Lloyd.

But one day, Yeti woke up and decided . . .

he liked making things . . .

more than he liked
breaking things.

So he built a little library.

And then a BIG one.

He befriended bees.

He told knock-knock jokes to the trees.

And he rehomed his fleas.

Yeti spent plenty of time alone . . .
but he wasn't lonely.

One evening when Yeti was cheering on the newly hatched baby sea turtles as they made their way to the ocean . . .

Lloyd came thundering up behind him and kicked the sand.

Yeti looked horrified and shook his head.

He offered Lloyd a kale chip instead.
Lloyd rolled his eyes and swatted the chip
out of Yeti's paw.

Yeti felt the hurtful sting of his words. He took a deep breath.
He counted to thirteen (his favorite number), and then he said . . .

Nothing.

Lloyd may have sixteen ears,
but he is a lousy listener.

The following day, everyone received an invitation to the annual Monster Bash & Barbecue.

Everyone except for Yeti, that is.

Was he disappointed? A little. After all, he had already made his famous seven-layer dip, the one Grimace was always so fond of wearing on her head every year.

"I know!" Yeti said. "I will throw a party of my own!"

He made invitations. He hung paper lanterns and paper cranes from the trees.

And he put on his favorite bow tie and record album.

The moon was Yeti's first guest to arrive.
The others soon followed.

Everyone had an excellent time. Especially Yeti.

In the distance, Yeti could hear the riotous sounds of the Monster Bash & Barbecue— dishes breaking, heads butting, and Lloyd shouting.

So he turned up the music.
Yes, it's true the world is full of monsters.
And Yeti.

For Hannah and Rick. Love wins.
—K.D.

To Henry and Olive.
—C.K.

VIKING
An imprint of Penguin Random House LLC, New York

First published in the United States of America by Viking, an imprint of Penguin Random House LLC, 2021

Text copyright © 2021 by Kelly DiPucchio
Illustrations copyright © 2021 by Claire Keane

Visit us online at penguinrandomhouse.com.

LIBRARY OF CONGRESS CATALOGING-IN-PUBLICATION DATA IS AVAILABLE.

Manufactured in China

ISBN 9780593114070

1 3 5 7 9 10 8 6 4 2

Design by Kate Renner
Text set in Clarendon LT Std

The art for this book was created using Photoshop.